HEAD, BODY, LEGS

A Story from Liberia

RETOLD BY

Won-Ldy Paye & Margaret H. Lippert

ILLUSTRATED BY Julie Paschkis

HENRY HOLT AND COMPANY ◆ NEW YORK

About the Story

Head, Body, Legs is a traditional creation story from
the Dan people of northeastern Liberia in Africa. Dan
mothers and grandmothers tell it to children to illustrate
the importance of cooperation—each part of the body is
necessary and helps the others, just as each person in a
family or a community is necessary and helps the others.

Henry Holt and Company, LLC
Publishers since 1866
115 West 18th Street
New York, New York 10011
Henry Holt is a registered trademark of Henry Holt and Company, LLC

Library of Congress Cataloging-in-Publication Data
Paye, Won-Ldy.
Head, body, legs: a story from Liberia / retold by Won-Ldy Paye
and Margaret H. Lippert; illustrated by Julie Paschkis.
Summary: In this tale from the Dan people of Liberia, Head, Arms,
Body, and Legs learn that they do better when they work together.
[1. Dan (African people)—Folklore. 2. Folklore—Liberia.]
I. Lippert, Margaret H. II. Paschkis, Julie, ill. III. Title.
PZ8.1.P24 He 2001   398.2   [E]—dc21   00-44856
ISBN 0-8050-6570-9 / First Edition—2002 / Designed by Martha Rago
The artist used Winsor & Newton gouaches to create the illustrations for this book.
Printed in the United States of America on acid-free paper. ∞

3 5 7 9 10 8 6 4 2

For my nieces and nephews in
Liberia and in the United States —W. P.

For Alan, Jocelyn, and Dawn
—M. H. L.

To Sam and Seiji
—J. P.

LONG AGO, Head
was all by himself.

He had no legs, no arms, no body. He rolled everywhere. All he could eat were things on the ground that he could reach with his tongue.

At night he rolled under a cherry tree. He fell asleep and dreamed of sweet cherries.

One morning
Head woke up and
thought, "I'm tired
of grass and mush-
rooms. I wish I could
reach those cherries."

He rolled himself up a
little hill. "Maybe if I get a good
head start I can hit the trunk hard
enough to knock some cherries
off," he thought. He shoved with his
ears and began to roll down the hill.
"Here I go!" he shouted.

Faster and faster he rolled.
CRASH!

"OWWWW!" he cried.

Head looked up. Above him swung two Arms he had never seen before.

"Look down here," Head said, "and you'll see."

"How can we look?" asked Arms. "We don't have eyes."

"I have an idea," said Head. "Let's get together. I have eyes to see, and you have hands for picking things to eat."

"Okay," said Arms. They dropped to the ground and attached themselves to Head above the ears.

"This," said Head, "is perfect."

Hands picked cherries,
and Head ate every single
one.

"It's time for
a nap," said Head,
yawning. Soon he
was fast asleep.

While Head slept, Body bounced along
and landed on top of him.

"Help!" gasped Head. "I can't breathe!"
Arms pushed Body off.

"Hey," said Body. "Stop pushing me.
Who are you?"

"It's us, Head and Arms," said Head.
"You almost squashed us. Watch where
you're going!"

"How can I?" asked Body. "I can't see."

"Why don't you join us?" said Head. "I see some ripe mangoes across the river. If you help us swim over there, I'll help you see where you're going."

"Okay," said Body. So Head attached himself to Body at the belly button.

"This," said
Head, "is perfect."

They bounced down the bank into the river. "Pull right . . . pull left," Head shouted to Arms, who paddled frantically against the current.

Soon they reached the far bank and bounced up to the mango tree.

"Pick some," Head ordered. Arms stretched as high as they could, but they couldn't quite reach. Head looked around for a stick. Standing near the tree were two crossed Legs with feet on the ends.

"Get those," Head said to Arms.

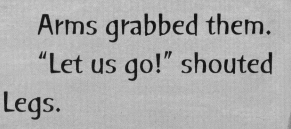

Arms grabbed them. "Let us go!" shouted Legs.

"Who are you?" asked Head. "We're Legs. We were walking but we bumped into this tree."

"Join us," said Head. "I have eyes. I can show you where to go, and you can help us reach those mangoes."

"Okay," said Legs. So Legs attached themselves to the hands.

"Not there," said Arms. "The hands need to be free to pick mangoes."

"I should be in the middle," said Body, "because I'm the biggest."

"That's right," said Head. "You should be at the bottom, Legs. I'll swing around on top of Body so I can see everything. And Arms, you move to the shoulders."

Everyone slid into place. Legs stood on tiptoe. Body straightened out. Arms stretched up, and the hands picked a mango. Head took a bite.

"Mmm, delicious," Head said.
"Now THIS is perfect!"